ROOPSTER ROUX *presents*

MODERN DAY Fairy Tales

RR
ROOPSTER
ROUX

FORWARD BY CYNTHIA COOPER

ILLUSTRATED BY VUTHY KUON EDITED BY LAVAILLE LAVETTE

HAJIMZEL • PROVIDENCE

In memory of Ngy Kuon

"I love you, Dad"

V.K.

Text copyright © 1999 by Providence Publishing
Illustrations copyright © 1999 by Vuthy Kuon
All rights reserved.
Published by Providence Pnblishing
4306 Brook Woods, Houston, TX 77092
For ordering information, call (888) 966-3833
Printed in China
Second Printing
10 9 8 7 6 5 4 3

Library of Congress Catalog Card Number 99-90030
Modern day fairy tales / Vuthy Kuon.
Summary: An anthology of rewritten fairy tales and nursery rhymes
by the winners of Roopster Roux's 1999 Young Authors Contest.
ISBN 0-9651661-1-2

Table of Contents

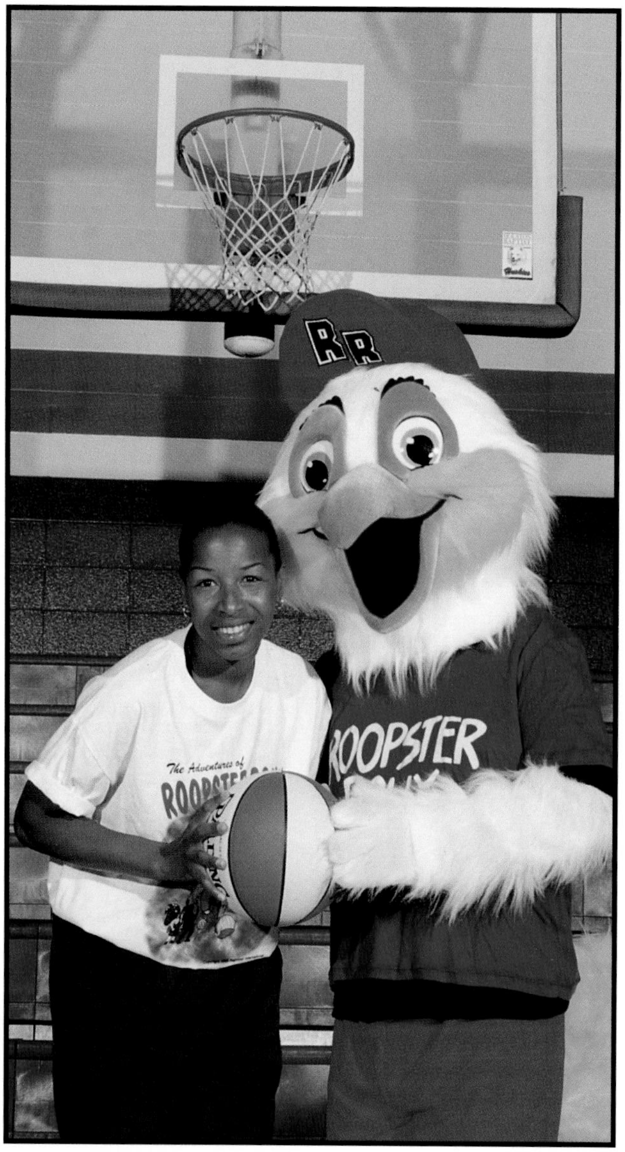
RR
ROOPSTER

Forward

by Cynthia Cooper

WNBA star Cynthia Cooper and that reading, sports-loving rooster, Roopster Roux, talk about Modern Day Fairy Tales.

Cynthia Cooper: Roopster, where did you find such great stories? I'm so excited that you asked me to help you introduce these stories by young writers.

Roopster Roux: Aren't they great? I'm so proud of them all.

Cynthia Cooper: I am too. All are talented writers. How did you find the stories?

Roopster Roux: We held the first annual Young Authors Writing Contest for children living in and around Houston, Texas.

Cynthia Cooper: That must have been fun. Did you get to read all the stories?

Roopster Roux: You bet! Hundreds of kids from 1st through 6th grade entered the contest. There were so many good stories, we had a hard time picking the winners. Three finalists were slam-dunks, and we had 10 stories that received honorable mentions.

Cynthia Cooper: Wow! These are really good stories.

Roopster Roux: They were so good, I want other kids to read them.

Cynthia Cooper: Readers will find all kinds of stories in this book. Some of the writers wrote new versions of old stories.

Roopster Roux: Like Michelle Pascoe's story "Sleeping Ugly" and "Humpty Dumpty" by Gabriel Castillo.

Cynthia Cooper: And don't forget "The Real Story of Little Red Riding Hood" by Phu Tran. He tells us the Wolf's version of the story. That was funny. And so was "Little Miss Muffet" by Jasmyne Williams. Did you know Little Miss Muffet likes pork beans and rice?

Roopster Roux: Yes, I liked that. And a new story of "Jack & Jill" by Victor Chavez that tells how Jack and Jill find a safe way to get water from the top of the hill.

Cynthia Cooper: I see some good poems, too.

Roopster Roux: Yes, there's a new lullaby, "Bye Baby Bunting" by Melissa Moore, and a whole story in poem, "Tommy Snooks and Bessy Brooks" by Chelsie Gonzales. A girl named Kary learns to move fast in "Kary Be Nimble" by Deandra Cooper.

Cynthia Cooper: I like the surprise ending in Jose Garza's "What Did She Do?" In "Cinderella," by Leslie Orllena, the Prince finds Cinderella in a new way.

Roopster Roux: That's right. And Tenisha Burks wrote a story, "Chiwaukathema & Prince Jester," with a magic spell in it. There's another story about magic, "The Dragon & the Unicorn" by George Perez. I know all the kids who read these stories will love them as much as I do.

Cynthia Cooper: I'm proud of the kids who are reading this book. I want everyone who reads this book to keep on reading others.

Roopster Roux: Me, too. Reading is very important. It's my favorite thing to do, along with sports.

Cynthia Cooper: I guess that's true for me, too. I love basketball, and I sure love to read.

Tommy Snooks & Bessy Brooks

by Chelsie Gonzales

As Tommy Snooks and Bessy Brooks were walking out one Sunday,
Says Tommy Snooks to Bessy Brooks, "Wilt you marry me on Monday?"

Says Bessy Brooks to Tommy Snooks, while walking out one Sunday,
"Oh yes I will, 'twould be a thrill, but maybe not on Monday!"

Says Bessy Brooks to Tommy Snooks, as they went out to play,
"What shall we dear, when Tuesday's here? 'Twill be my sewing day!"

Says Tommy Snooks to Bessy Brooks, as they raced across the floor,
"Wednesday's no good, I don't think we should. I've got to do my chores!"

Says Bessy Brooks to Tommy Snooks, as they were having tea,
"Oh, boo hoo, Thursday won't do! My father wilt go out to sea!"

Says Tommy Snooks to Bessy Brooks, as they peered through the garden gate,
"Friday I cannot, to town I must trot and shan't be home until late!"

Says Bessy Brooks to Tommy Snooks, as they were eating pie,
"On Saturday, I was to play just Sally Sue and I!"

Says Tommy Snooks to Bessy Brooks after Sunday church they'd been,
"Forget the dream, let's get ice cream and race toward home again!"

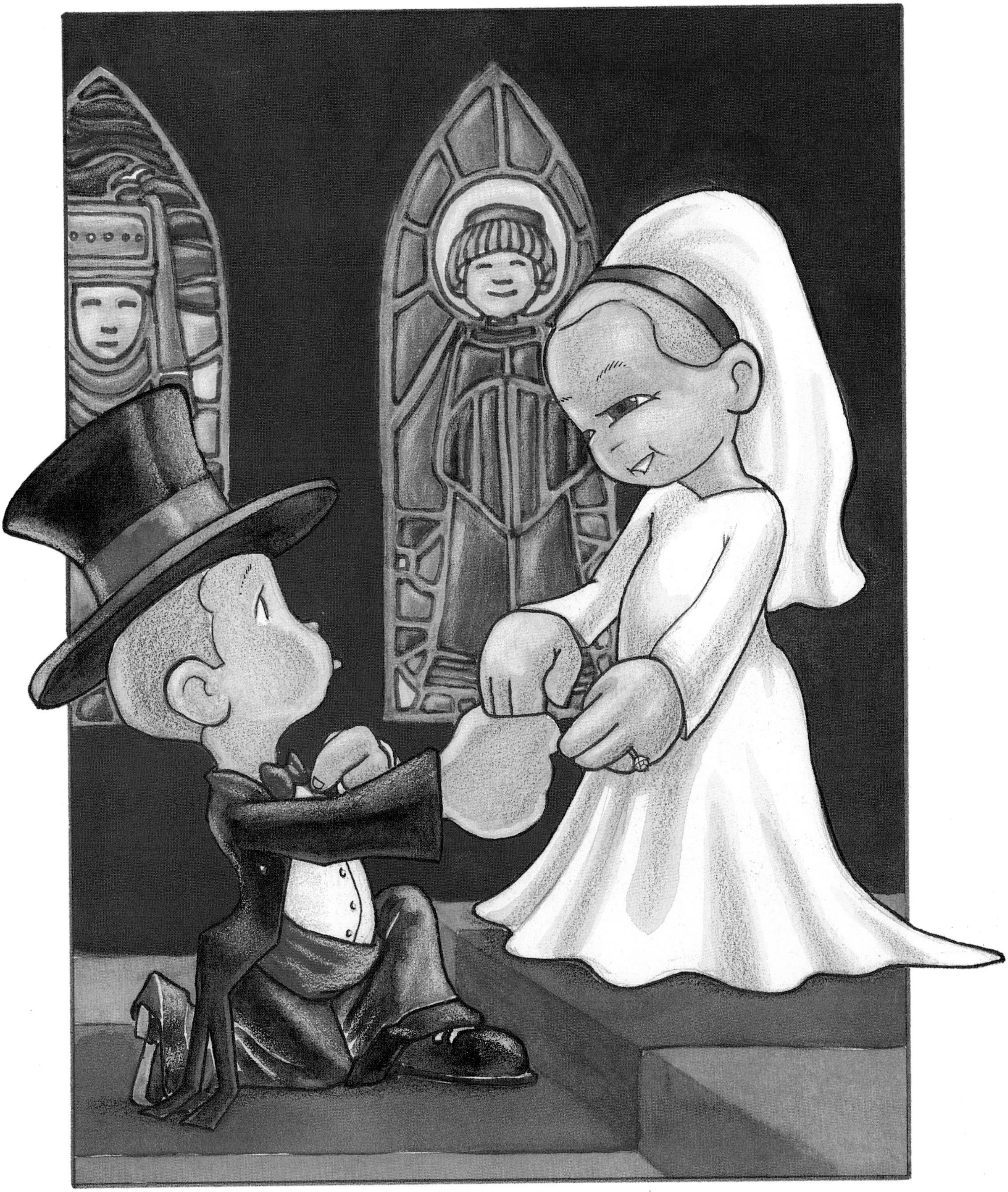

HUMPTY DUMPTY

by Gabriel R. Castillo

Once upon a time there was a little boy named Humpty Dumpty. He sat on a wall and heard some music, so he stood up and started dancing. Since Humpty was not a very good dancer, he fell off and started rolling down the street.

He first rolled over Little Red Riding Hood, then the Three Little Pigs and every other fairy tale and nursery rhyme character out on the streets that day. He kept rolling and rolling until... he crashed into some garbage cans!

His mother found his shell cracked and called the ambulance. When the doctor arrived, he ran a series of tests, checked his pulse, and told her, " I'm sorry ma'am, your son has a bad case of salmonella."

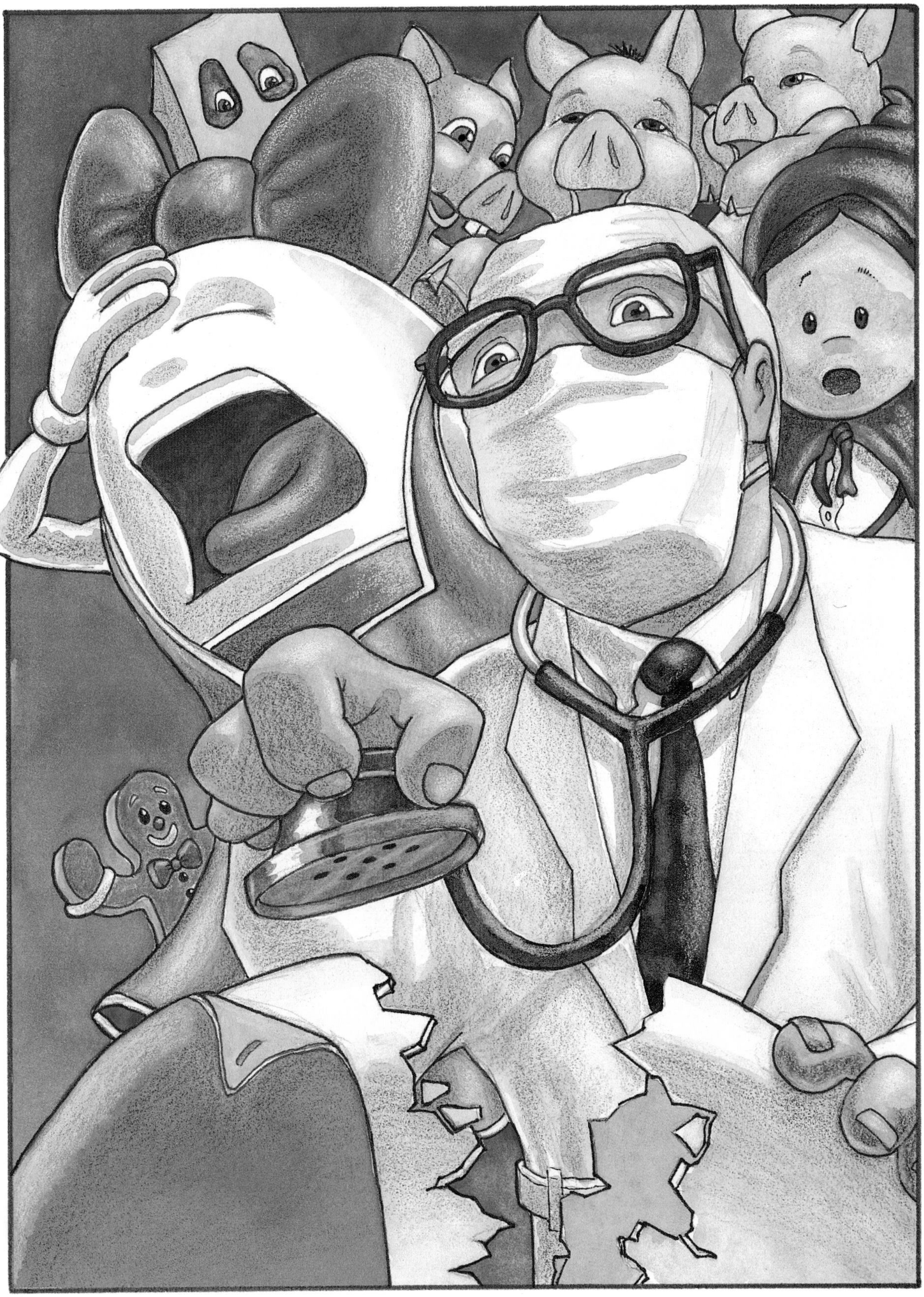

BYE BABY BUNTING

by Melissa Moore

Father's a-going to buy a car seat.
   Granny's a-cookin' some meat.
Great Gramma a-sittin' in the heat.
   And I'm a-rockin' Baby Bunting to the beat.

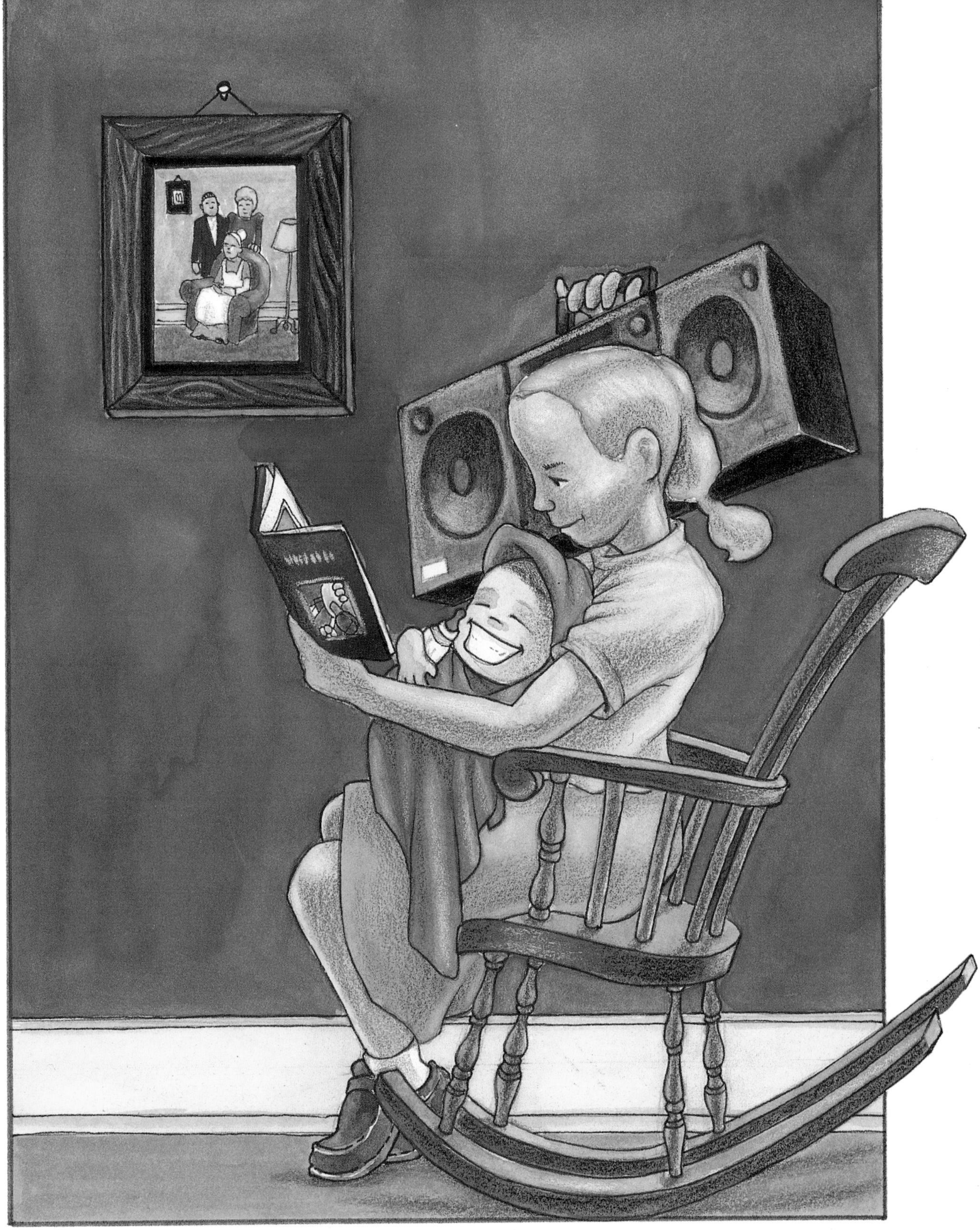

LITTLE MISS MUFFET

by Jasmyne Williams

Little Miss Muffet sat on her puppet, eating pork beans and rice.
The puppet cried out, "Hey, get off of me!"
And Miss Muffet spilled her pork beans and rice.

Miss Muffet screamed, as she sat on that rock.
She had never heard her puppet talk.
She just cleaned her dress, and went for a walk.

Then she looked behind her and saw a pack of wolves. She wondered where these wolves came from. Pretty soon they started growling at her because she had a pork beans and rice stain on her dress. She started running until she came to her secret route, the same one she took every day after school. She was finally able to get away from the wolves. Then she sat down on the nearest bench and said, "They were trying to get the pork beans and rice from my dress. This time I'm just going to eat curds and whey." She heard a loud noise which made her spill curds and whey on her dress. She wondered what it was, so she looked up and she saw a Tarantula!

Not again!" she cried and ran out of sight.

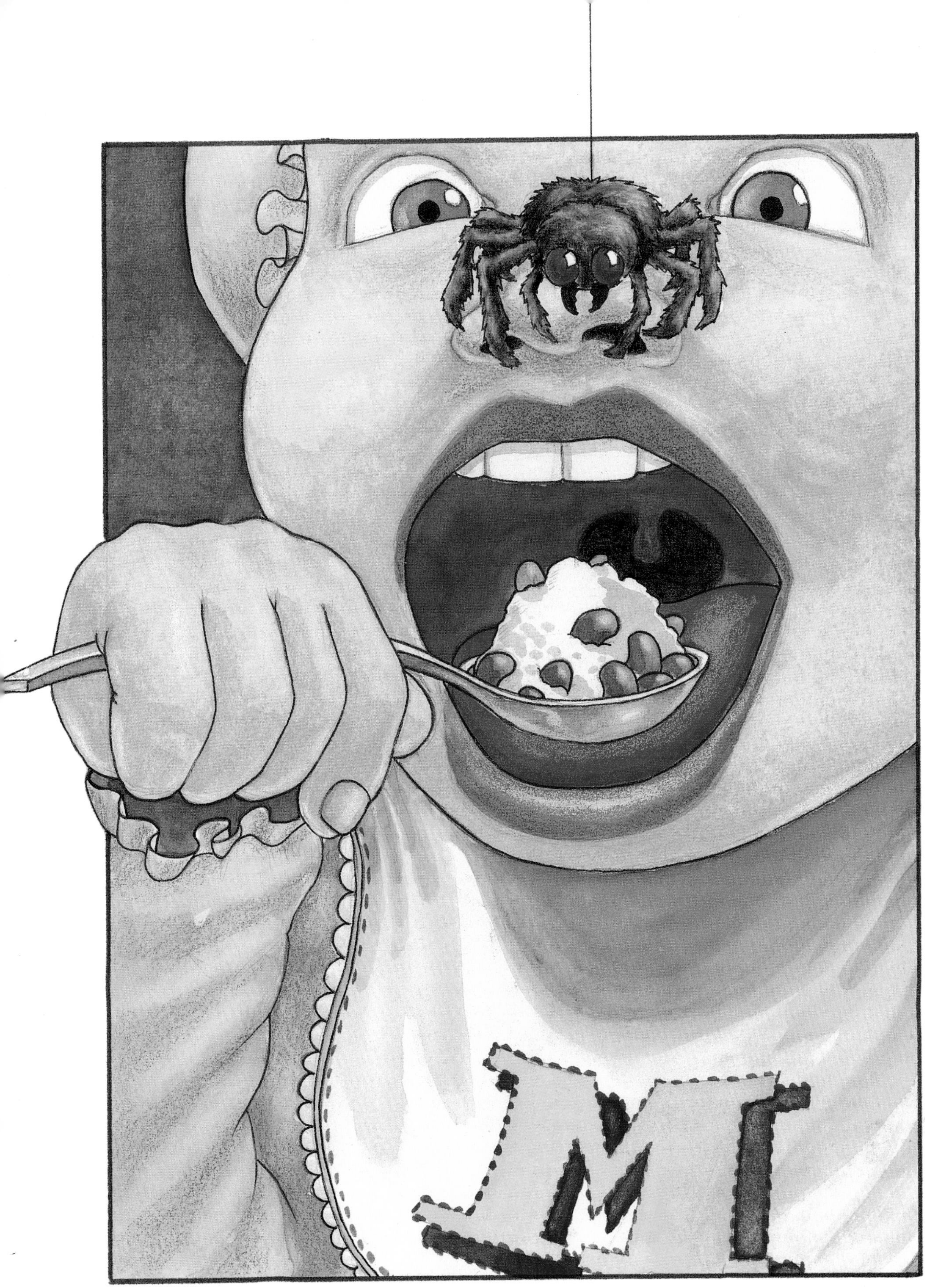
M

KARY BE NIMBLE

by Deandra Cooper

Kary be nimble, Kary be quick.

   Kary jumped over a big broomstick.

Kary jumped high, and then skipped low.

   Kary broke... her big toe.

Kary skipped fast and then skipped slow.

   Kary ran into a garden hoe...

   ... and broke... her little toe.

Kary ran here and she ran there.

   Kary ran into a big brown bear.

The bear ate Kary's poison hair.

   The people said,

 "Yeah, the brown bear's dead."

Kary closed her eyes and went to bed.

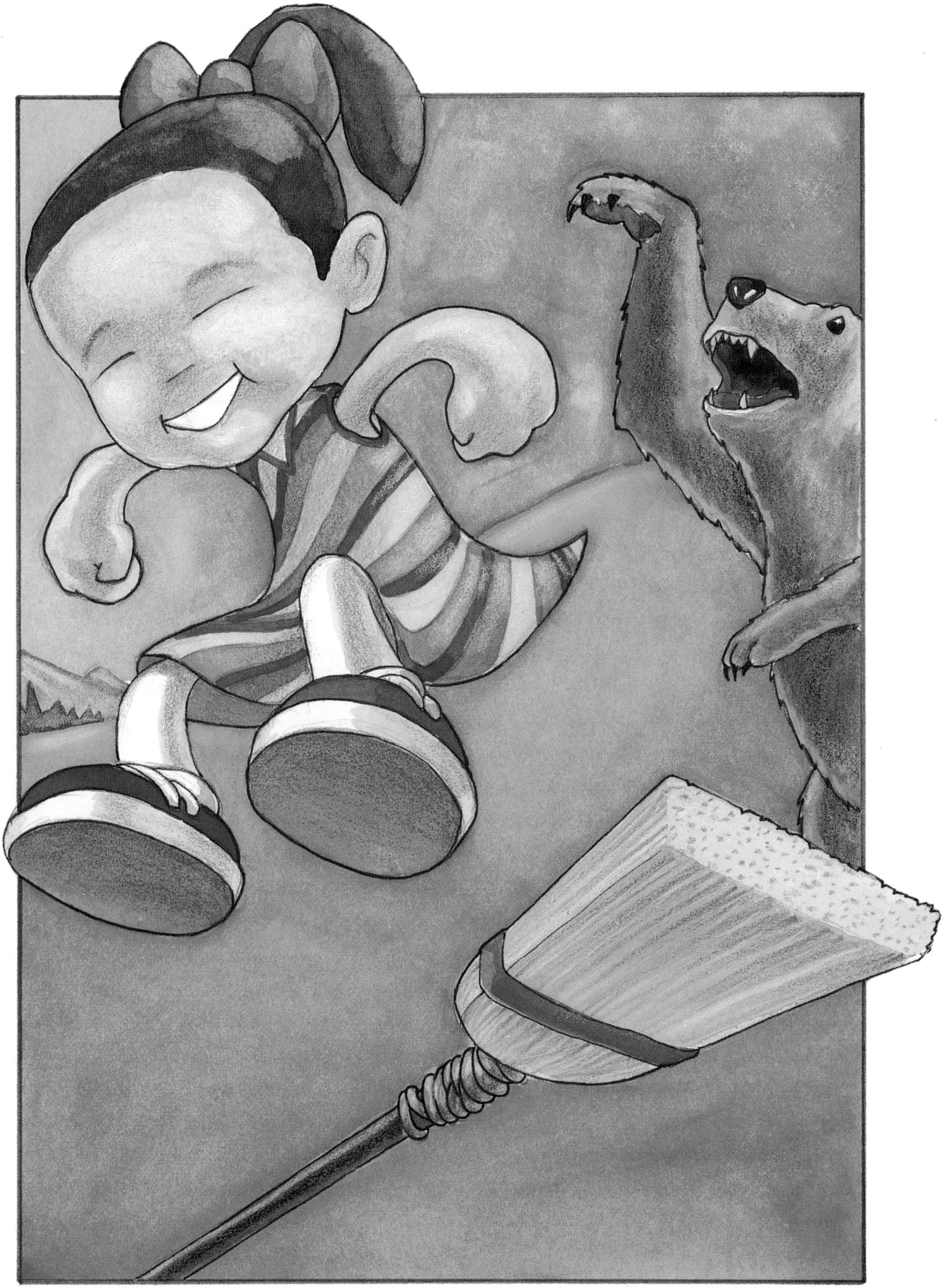

THE GINGERBREADMAN

by Gabriel Vasquez

Once upon a time an old lady named Granny made a gingerbread man. The Gingerbread Man had a white mouth, white eyes, a red nose and three buttons. When the Gingerbread Man was ready, he popped out of the pan, dashed into Granny's car, and drove away.

"Stop!" shouted the old lady, but he wouldn't stop driving.

A farmer saw the Gingerbread Man running away and he yelled, "Stop!" but the Gingerbread Man still would not stop driving.

A dog saw him driving away in the car and the dog hollered, "Stop!" but he kept on driving.

Later a little boy saw him running away.

"Stop!" Shouted the granny.

"Stop!" hollered the farmer.

"Stop!" said the dog.

"Stop!" shouted the little boy, but the Gingerbread Man did not stop driving. The Gingerbread Man kept driving, but stopped when he came to a lake. He spotted a giant alligator that looked like a bridge to the other side. He looked back again and Granny was still there... so was the farmer and the little boy. The Gingerbread Man got out of the car and jumped on the alligator's tail, then his back, then his head, then his nose! Then the alligator sneezed and threw him to Mexico. He landed in a volcano and the Gingerbread Man burned to a crisp.

Now nobody will ever chase him down again because nothing tastes worse than burnt gingerbread.

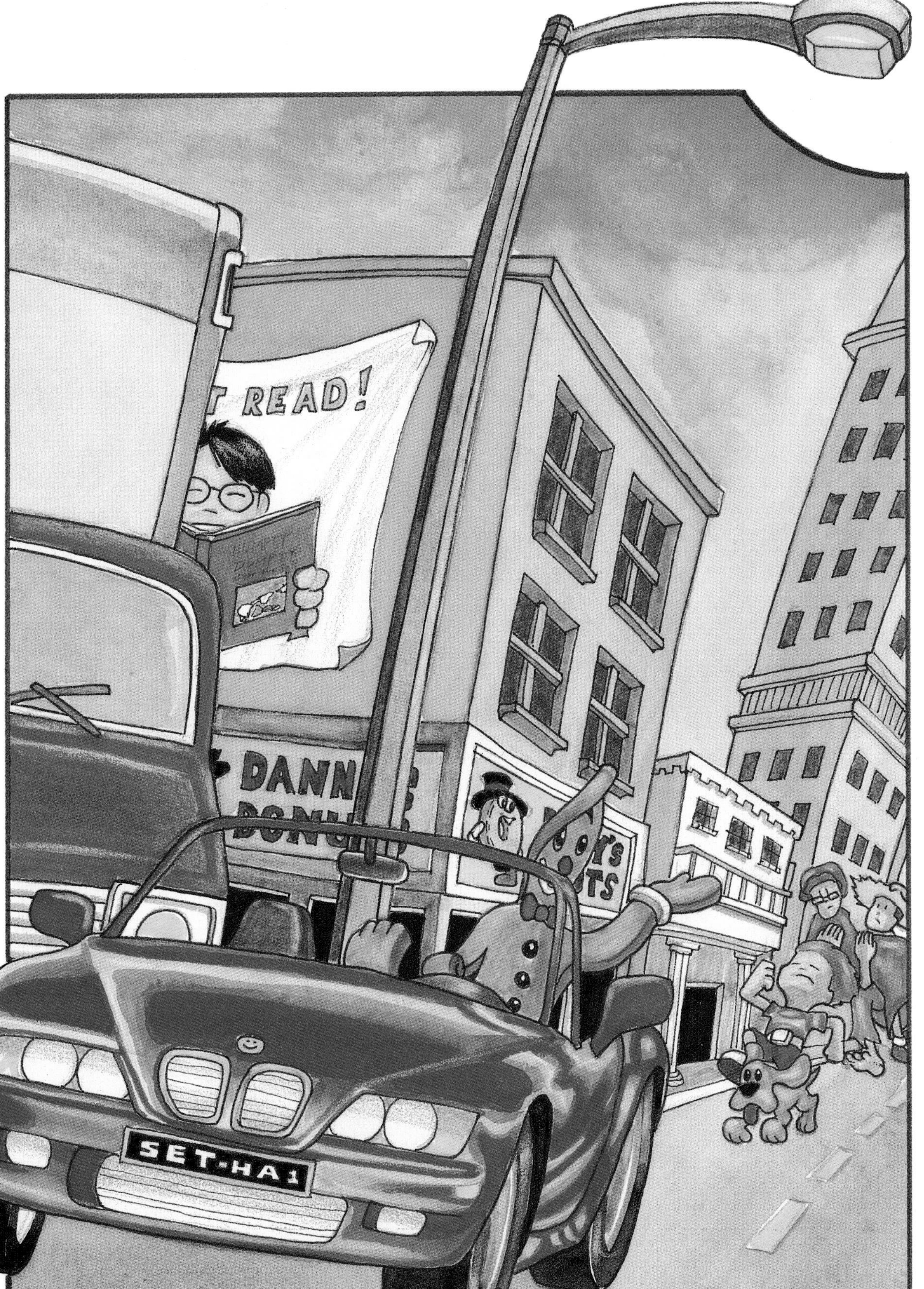
READ!
SET-HA1

CINDERELLA (translated from Spanish)

by Leslie Orllena

Once upon a time there lived a muchacha named Cinderella. She lived with her stepmother and dos wicked stepsisters. She was bonita, sensilla, and generosa, so her stepsisters were jealous of her. Un dia, Cinderella asked her stepmother if she could go to the ball, and her stepmother told her, "The way you look, nadie will to want to dance with you! You are going to stay in the casa... cleaning!" Cinderella stayed behind... llorando. Her fairy godmother heard this, so she waved her magic varita, dressed her in a gorgeous vestido with shiny zapatos, and also made a beautiful coche with strong caballos. Before she sent her off, her fairy godmother warned her that she has to return before midnight or she would become a piedra!

Cinderella went to the ball and was the most beautiful muchacha there. She caught the prince's ojo and they danced all night long. She was having so much fun that she didn't realize that it was tres minutos before midnight! She ran off quickly and dropped her diamond arete. The prince chased her, picked up the lost arete and announced, "The muchacha who has the other arete will be mi esposa." The prince searched through the whole kingdom and nobody had the arete. The stepmother's castillo was the final one on the list, so he knocked on the puerta and asked, "Do any of you have the other arete?" Nadie lo tenia. So as the prince turned to leave, he saw a sparkle coming from inside the cocina. There he found Cinderella dormiendo... and on her oido shined the matching arete! The prince gently put the missing arete on her other oido and asked her in a soft voz, "Nos casaremos?" Cinderella vio para arriba and with lagrimas in her ojos, she said, "Si." Despues se casaron y tuvieron una hija que nombraron... Cinderella.

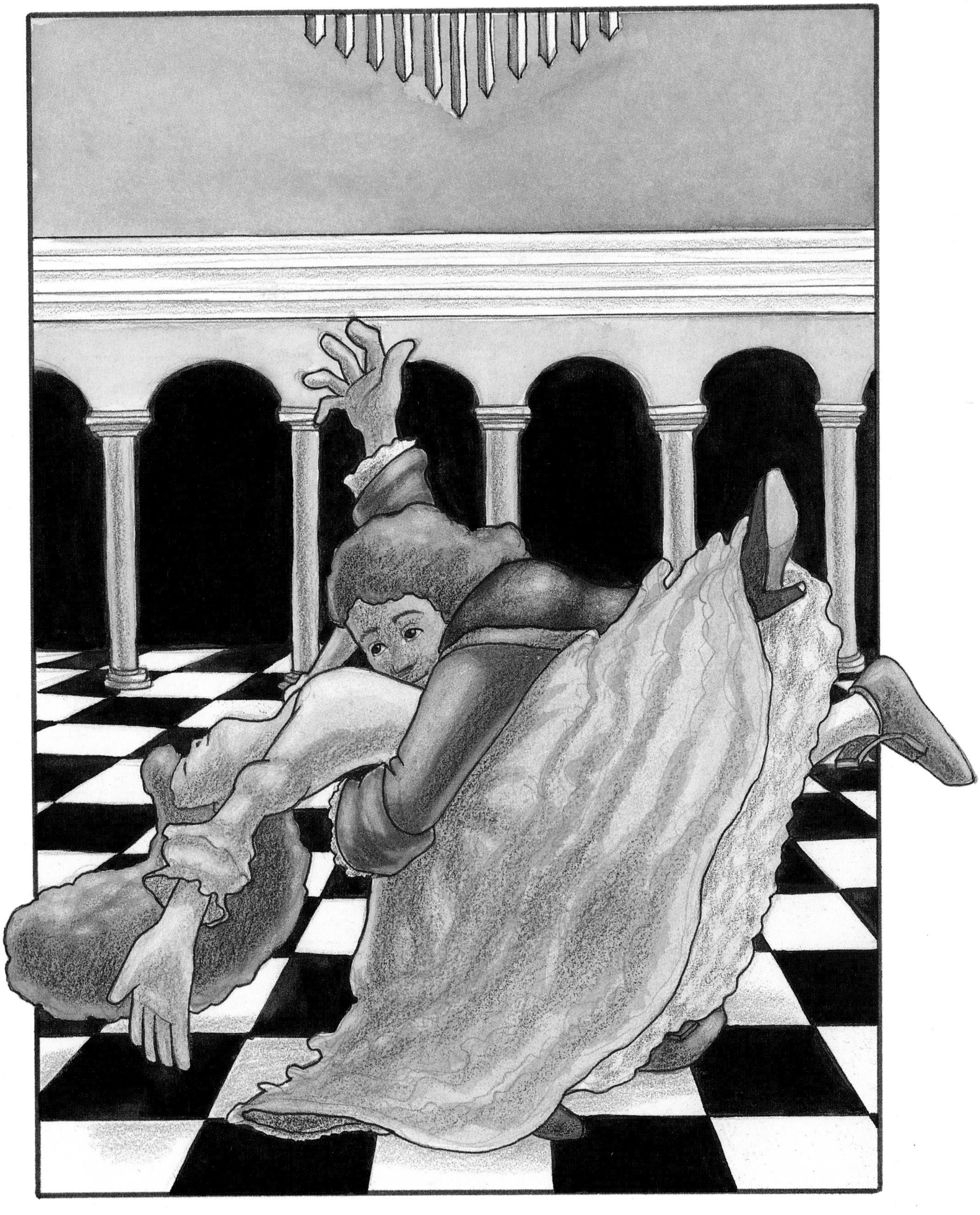

THE REAL STORY OF LITTLE RED RIDING HOOD

by Phu Tran

Hi, my name is Joe, the wolf. I'm the bad guy in the story, "Little Red Riding Hood." I was accused and framed for the "grandma incident," and now I want to explain my side of the story. This is what really happened...

I was walking through the forest minding my business until I bumped into Little Red Riding Hood holding a basket. Then out of her basket, a piece of paper slipped out and landed in my paw. It read, "How to get rid of Grandma." Concerned about poor old grandma, I persuaded Little Red to go the long way, so I arrived at grandma's first. I tried to tell grandma about her fate, but of course, who would believe a wolf? I tried to hide her, but it was too late. Little Red was knocking on the door. Running out of choices, I decided to hide Grandma in my stomach. I dressed up in her clothes and planned to stop Little Red. She came in with a big grin on her face and started asking me these weird questions. She talked for quite a while... a real motor mouth... but finally she turned around and there was my chance to grab the basket. I crept carefully towards her, and just when I was about to snatch it, she turned around and saw me. I chuckled nervously and froze. Thinking that I was going to eat her, she hit me with the basket. WHAP! The next thing I knew, I saw stars of many kinds.

When I came to, I was in the slammer. I tried and tried to tell them and again, who would believe a wolf? Poor Grandma. Well, that's my story, and now you know what really happened. So don't believe what others say. I've done my time and here I am at home, relaxing and telling you my story. Oops! I'm late for the Hood Family Reunion to remember grandma. I don't know why they invited me. Bye!

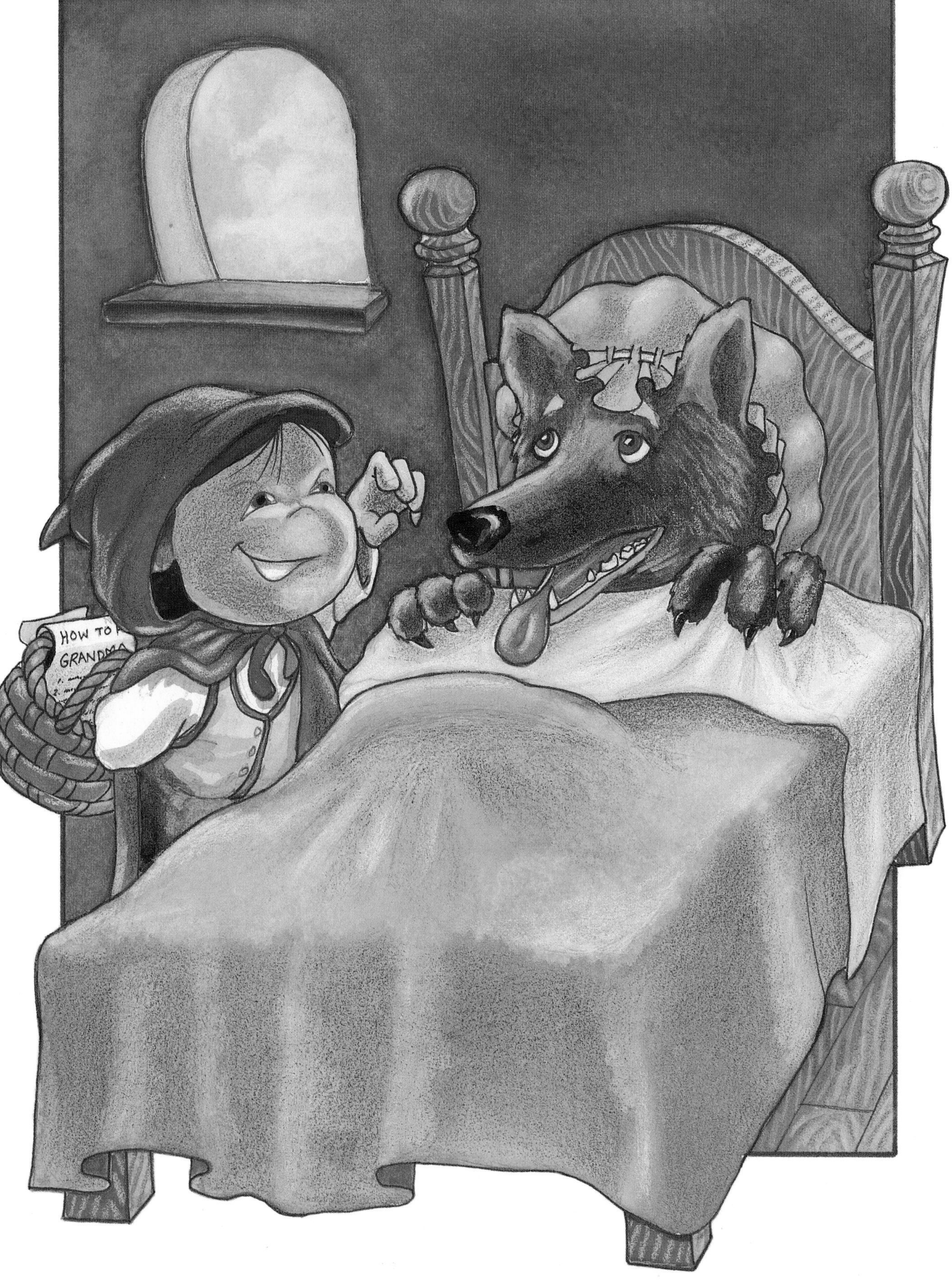
HOW TO
GRANDMA

SLEEPING UGLY

by Michelle Pascoe

There once was a princess named Sleeping Ugly. She was so ugly that not even her mother could look at her... so she ran away.

In the forest, she saw a cottage that had a witch in it. She did not know the lady was a witch, so she yelled out bad things to her. Of course the witch did not want to help her, so she walked farther away into the forest, where she met an even uglier boy. They started to talk and get to know each other better.

They decided to go rock climbing and became a little nicer looking to each other. After that, they went to a movie and became even more good looking. So every time they did something together, they became better looking than before.

About thirty years later, they became so good looking that they got married and had two ugly babies.

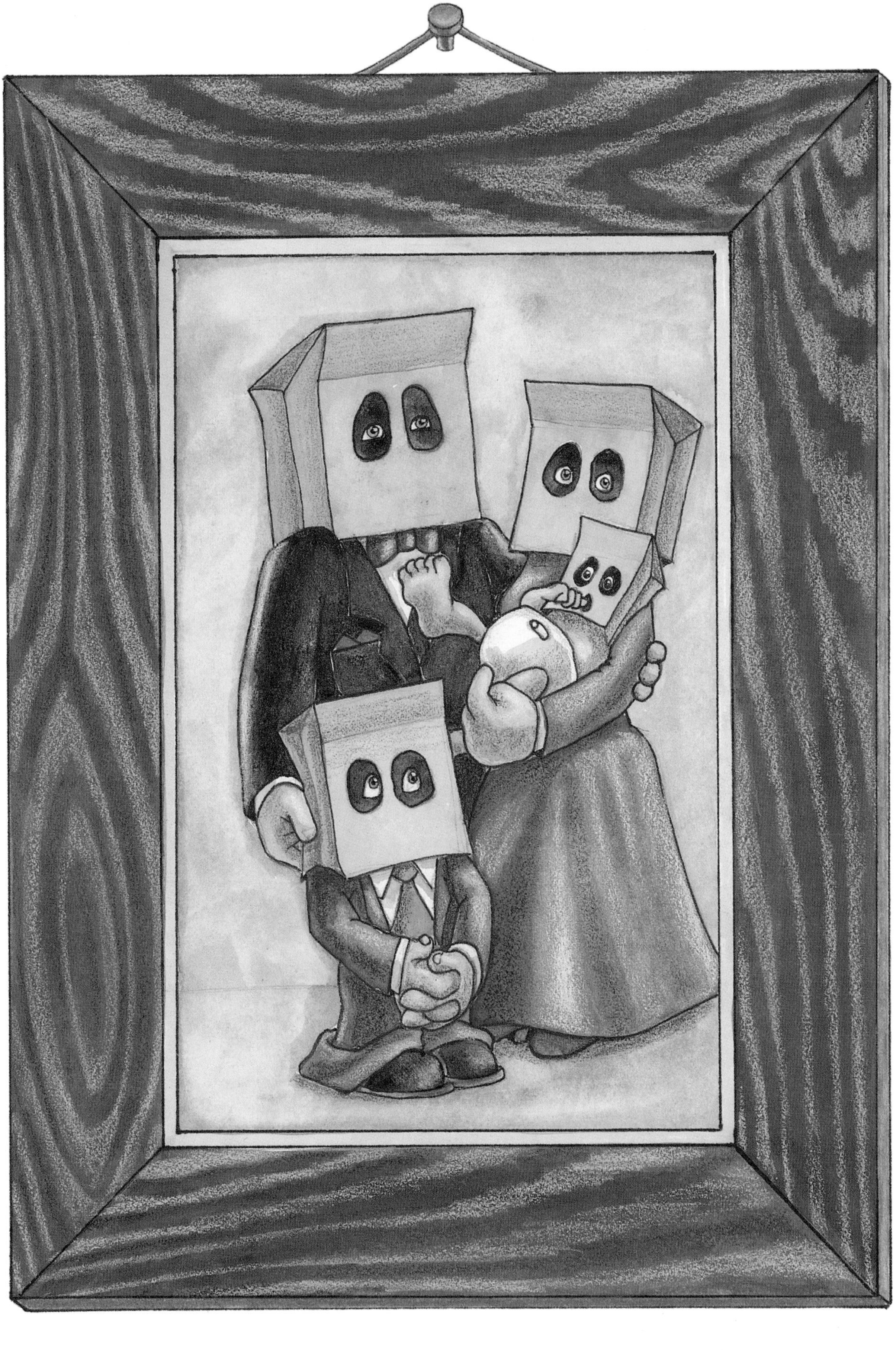

Jack & Jill

by Victor Chavez

Jack and Jill went up the hill to fetch a pail of water. Jack fell down and broke his crown and Jill came tumbling after.

Dr. David helped Jack get home. He put medicine on his head, gave him aspirin for his headache, then he wrapped Jack's head with long strips of bandages.

When Jack recovered, he told Jill, "We have to get water from the hill and I have a plan. Let's go to the zoo and get a tiger. He can carry us up the hill together." And so they did. They started up the hill but they did not get far before the tiger got tired and stopped. When the tiger stopped they all slid back down the hill.

Jack had to think of another plan. Jack decided to get a motorcycle. They rode up the hill but the brakes went out, so they could not stop. The motorcycle went right back down the hill. Once again, Jack and Jill came down without a pale of water. Jack had to think of another plan.

Jack called and asked the president if he could use a bald eagle. The eagle grabbed Jack and Jill with its feet and carried them up the hill. They fetched the water and the eagle took them home. Jack and Jill shared the water with the eagle. After that, whenever they needed help, they knew they could always count on the bald eagle.

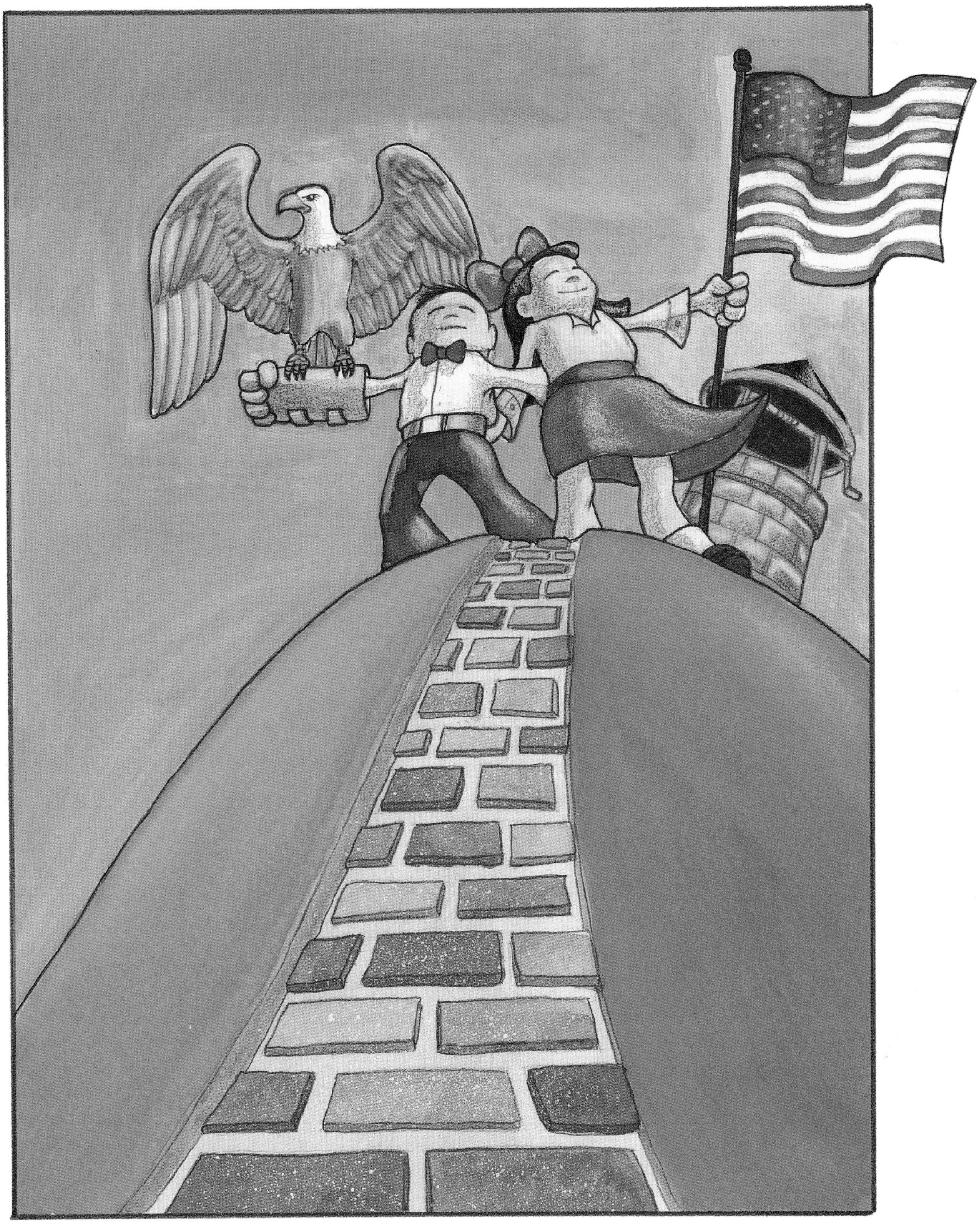

THE DRAGON & THE UNICORN

by George Perez

Once in a forsaken jungle there lived a peaceful dragon, but when you get him mad he isn't so peaceful. The dragon's best friend was a unicorn. They loved to destroy trees together. As a geologist, I was sent to explore the jungle. The unicorn saw me and told the dragon that there was a delicious morsel up ahead, so they chased me! Up ahead I saw a red colored tent, and I went in it for safety. I found out that I was not alone. A wizard appeared and said to me, "You are in grave danger! Let me guess, a dragon and a unicorn are chasing you, right?"

"Yes, how did you know?" I asked.

"Just listen! Take this antidote, drink it and stand up to those carnivores," the wizard said.

"CARNIVORES?" I said in a scared voice.

"You will be immortal for about five weeks if you take the antidote. If you defeat them you will become a god!" the wizard told me. I cautiously took the antidote and looked for the biggest object I could carry. The unicorn tried to stab me with his horn. I hit the unicorn with the massive tree branch I had found and knocked off his horn. The unicorn fell and gradually dissolved. The dragon became not so friendly because I defeated his best friend, so I kicked him in the stomach. He wasn't dead, just hurt bad. I grabbed the branch and stuck it in his mouth just as he was about to breathe fire. The dragon instantly inflated like a balloon and he blew up... along with the wizard's tent! A strong beam of light struck me and before I knew it, I took Zeus's place up in the heavens.

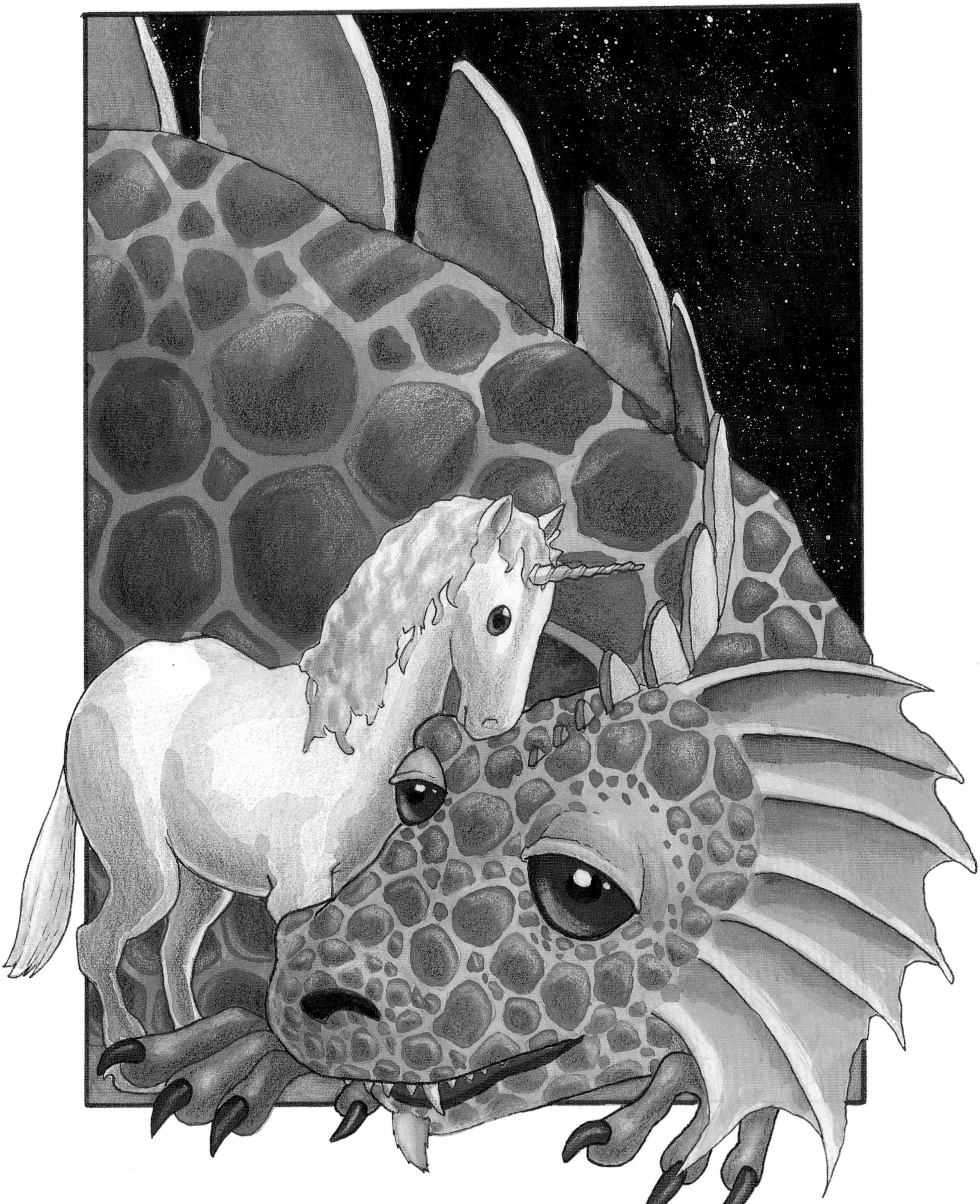

CHIWAUKATHEMA & PRINCE JESTER

by Tenisha Burks

Once upon a time in a town named Playaville, there lived a prince named Jester. Prince Jester lived in a huge castle willed to him by his deceased father. Prince Jester was so lonely that one day he decided to start a search for a beautiful young woman to be his bride.

In the near village lived two single women. While on a walk, one of the young women, Chiwaukathema, found a notice that read: "Prince Jester is looking for a beautiful woman to soon be his princess. His Royal Highness expects all young women to be at his castle Saturday at midnight."

Chiwaukathema went and told her sisters. Quefundelan, the sweet and kind sister, thought it would be great if Chiwaukathema met the prince. But Afthena, the evil and unkind sister, said she would meet the prince before Chiwaukathema. That night, Afthena decided to cast a spell on Chiwaukathema that would weaken Chiwaukathema, so she herself could meet the prince. Afthena didn't know Chiwaukathema was watching her. By the time Afthena fell asleep, Chiwaukathema went to reverse the spell.

At midnight, Chiwaukathema was ready to meet the prince. When Afthena awakened, she was very weak. Chiwaukathema had already arrived at the castle where she met the prince. He took her hand for a dance. The next morning, Chiwaukathema and the prince were married. Luckily, the spell wasn't strong enough to do permanent damage to Afthena, but she did learned that being selfish to others leads her nowhere but to danger. From that day forward, Prince Jester and Princess Chiwaukathema lived happily ever after.

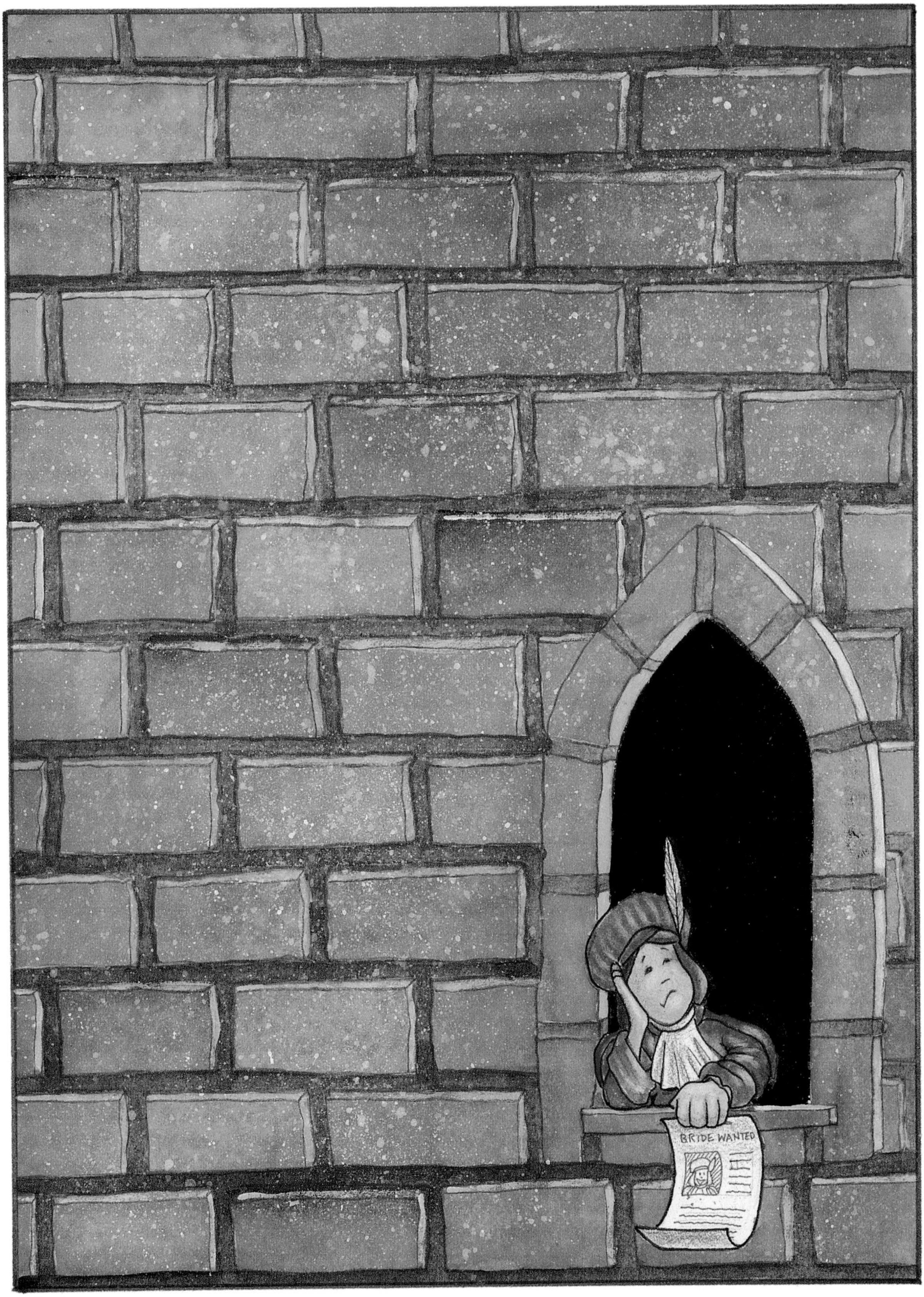
BRIDE WANTED

What Did She Do?

by Jose Garza

There was an old lady that lived in a shoe.

She had so many children, she didn't know what to do...

...so she called the babysitters and went on vacation to China.

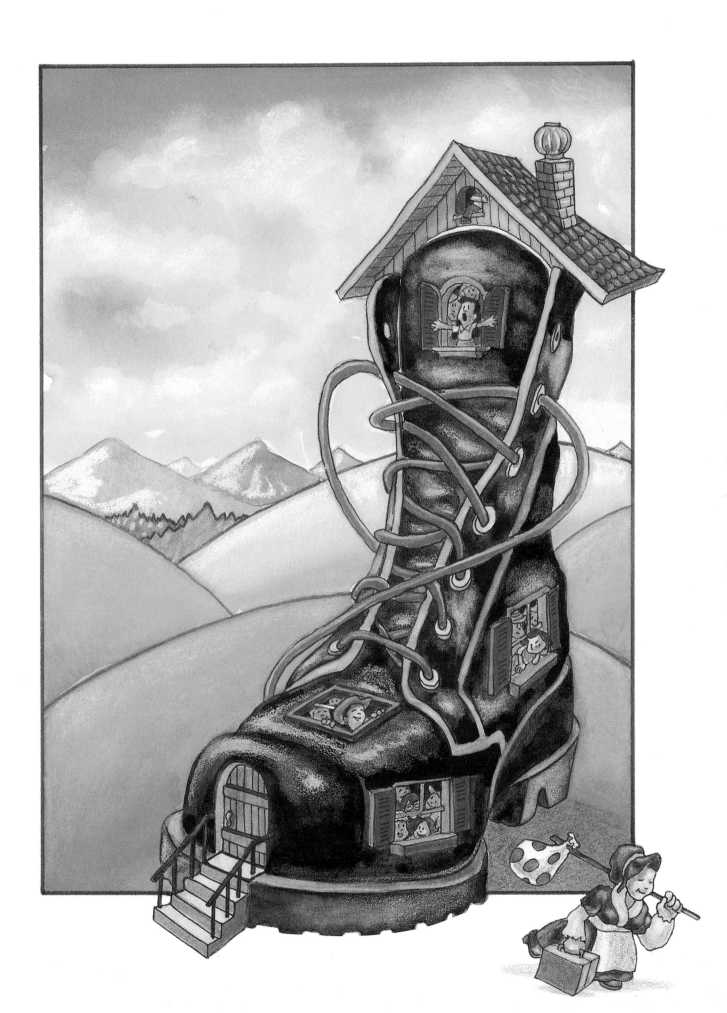

ABOUT THE AUTHORS

(current to the time of book production)

Chelsie Gonzales won the gold medal for the Roopster Roux 1999 Young Author's Writing Contest. Chelsie, a home-schooled student, is 10 years old and is in 5th grade at Eagles Way Christian. Her family of four lives in Pearland, Texas where she enjoys reading, writing, singing, stamp collecting, and beanie babies.

Gabriel R. Castillo is the silver medalist for this year's contest. He, too, is 10 years old and is in 5th grade at J.D. Ryan Elementary of the Houston Independent School District (HISD). Gabriel has three siblings and currently resides in Houston, Texas.

Melissa Ann Moore is the youngest of the three medalists. She won the bronze medal as a 3rd grader at Charlotte B. Allen Elementary (HISD) while only 9 years old. Melissa's interests include math, reading, social studies, science, and bike riding. Melissa is a resident of Houston, Texas.

Jasmyne Williams attends Alcott Elementary (HISD). She is 11 years old and in the 6th grade. Jasmyne loves skating, computers, and swimming.

Deandra Cooper attends M.C. Williams Middle School (HISD) as a 6th grader. She is 11 years old and has 3 siblings. Deandra lives in Houston and enjoys running.

Gabriel Vasquez is a 6th grader at Edison Middle School (HISD). He is 11 years of age and likes drawing, rollerblading, football, baseball, and video games.

Leslie Orllena is our only winner who wrote her story in Spanish, then it was translated to English. She is a 4th grader at Emerson Elementary (HISD) who likes to draw, paint, and do math.

Phu Cao Tran attends Lanier Middle School (HISD) as a 6th grader. This talented 12-year old enjoys playing sports, drawing, writing, and reading fantasy books.

Michelle Megan-Jayne Pascoe is one of seven children. She is a 4th-grader at Holden Elementary (HISD). She likes soccer, reading, writing, drawing, and movies.

Victor Hugo Chavez is 10 years old, attending 4th grade at Ethel R. Coop Elementary (HISD). Victor collects old model cars, plays soccer, and writes poetry.

George Perez likes to read, play video games, and collect toy cars. He is 11 and attends Brookline Elementary (HISD) as a 5th-grader. He has 3 siblings.

Tenisha Roshae Burks attends Watkins Junior High in the Cy-Fair Independent School District. She is 13 years old and loves singing, poetry, and basketball.

Jose Garza is the youngest of all our winners, having just finished 1st grade when he wrote his story. He attends Durkee Elementary (HISD) and enjoys basketball and street hockey.